Losing It

Roger Granelli

D0586972

ACCENT PRESS LTD

Published by Accent Press Ltd – 2008

ISBN 9781906125943

The Quick Reads project in Wales is a joint venture between Basic
Skills Cymru and the Welsh Books Council. Titles are funded through
Basic Skills Cymru as part of the National Basic Skills Strategy for
Wales on behalf of the Welsh Assembly Government.

Printed and bound in the UK

Cover design by The Design House

**CYNGOR LLYFRAU CYMRU
WELSH BOOKS COUNCIL**

Noddir gan
Lywodraeth Cynulliad Cymru
Sponsored by
Welsh Assembly Government

**Words Talk-Numbers Count
Geiriau'n Galw-Rhifau'n Cyfri**

Quick Reads ™ used under licence

Chapter One

As Baldock made his plans he tried to keep a clear head. Revenge was worth waiting for – a dish best served up cold. He'd read that in a book once. Baldock wanted to get even with TJ, and it was necessary to get even with TJ, but he had to maintain his cool, no matter how hard this was. People would be watching. His reputation was on the line.

Baldock liked his revenge hot and sudden – he'd lost it many times in the past, using his fists before his brain started up. When he found out what TJ had been doing he'd wanted to wring the little runt's neck, but instead he took a deep breath. Baldock took lots of deep breaths, and told himself to take it easy. There was no rush. In a way he almost admired TJ for having the bottle to rip him off. The little sod must have been desperate.

Baldock had his empire to consider, built up over ten years without the police ever getting a sniff. They'd picked up plenty of TJs over the years but none of them had led back to him. No one talked in this neck of the woods. Baldock was The Man now, and had been for some time. He liked to think of his world as an empire, a place where there was order, created by himself, a world where he was boss, number one. He had respect and fear. He had attention. Baldock had most of what he wanted in his life. Most, but not all. Karen had made sure of that.

Baldock stood by the bedroom window of his terraced house, looking out on the street, lost in his thoughts, until his father's husk of a voice interrupted them.

'You're like a bloody statue,' the old man said, 'standing there all the time. Worse than your mother ever was.'

Baldock turned round to look at the man swamped in bedclothes, propped up with pillows, once powerfully built, now all bones and cough. His father's eyes were still full of life though, and they flashed angrily at him now.

'You haven't eaten your food,' Baldock said.

'Don't want it. Rabbit food, that is.'

'You know what the doc said. It's what you're supposed to have.'

'What does it matter what I eat now? It's as stupid as trying to getting me to stop smoking. I've lived long enough, I reckon.'

'Don't start that again. You got a good few years yet. I'll make you a pot of tea. You never say no to that.'

Baldock tried to rearrange his father's pillows.

'Don't fuss, mun. For a big, hard lump, you're like an old woman sometimes.'

Baldock gave up and took his father's tray. He bent down close to the old man. His father smelt of a lifetime of smoking, and his face showed a lifetime of work. Old work, the type unknown by people Baldock's age. His father was marked up with old mining scars, lining his face and hands like blue tattoos. Baldock knew they were all over his body as well. He could just about remember, when he was a young kid, the old man coming home covered in dust sometimes because he couldn't be bothered to use the pit baths, and his mother washing him in the bath – the old-fashioned way, the way his father liked. That was a long time ago. The last pit in his area had closed before Baldock had left school, and he was only a few years off forty now.

'It's your birthday next week, Dad,' Baldock said. 'Eighty-two.'

'I know how old I am. It's my body that's worn out, not my head. Aye, I'm eighty-two and you're thirty-bloody-eight and still looking out the sodding window.'

Baldock smiled. He liked the old man's temper. It had lost some of its bite and could no longer be backed up by fists, but it was still there. Baldock had inherited it. This brought him round to TJ again. He could see the silly little sod showing off down the 'Bush, until he realised what he'd done and got scared. Very scared.

'I'll bring up the tea in a minute,' Baldock said. 'Oh, there's boxing on the telly.'

'Boxing, be buggered. That's not what I'd call it.'

The old man snatched up the TV remote and pointed it at the television, which Baldock had mounted on the wall. His father had been a decent fighter himself once, going from working at the coalface to attacking other men in the ring.

Baldock went downstairs to the kitchen to make the tea. There was a knock on the door.

'Is that you, Tony?' Baldock shouted.

The back door opened and Sharp Tony entered. He was called 'sharp' because he always wore the latest gear. 'I get it as quick as those London gits,' he liked to tell people. If you wanted to know what was in fashion, you looked at Tony. He was Baldock's main man, and Baldock trusted him, as much as he trusted anyone, which was not too much.

'You're late,' Baldock said.

'I know, boss, I had to wait around for the money,' Tony answered. 'You know what they're like up the site. Specially Maisy.'

'But no trouble?'

'Nah. As if. They're all talking 'bout TJ, though. Wondering what you gonna do, like.'

'What do you think I'm going to do?'

Tony grinned, showing an even set of teeth with two missing in the middle. It spoiled the effect of his new jacket.

'I don' wanna go there, boss. You know I'm the nervous type.'

'Any news on the little bastard?'

'TJ? Nah. Just that he's gone to ground, since the word is out. But all the boys is looking for the git.'

'Good.'

Baldock took the money from Tony and counted out two hundred notes. He gave him thirty back and went to his goods tin. He'd had it from the start, an old toffee tin of his mother's, matt black with a picture of two dogs on it. It was almost as old as Baldock. Tony was the only runner who was allowed to see it. It was usually kept in a hole behind one of the kitchen cupboards, but tonight Baldock had it on the table waiting. Tony's eyes kept flicking towards it, like a fox looking at chickens. Baldock opened the tin and took out the neatly prepared wraps of skunk.

'These are for the bottom site and Friday night. Give half to Rob and tell him to move himself. I've heard he's been spending most of his time in the club.'

'Right.'

Tony pushed a wrap against his nose and sniffed deeply.

'Good stuff, this is. The best we've had for ages, boss.'

'Is it?'

'Oh aye, I forget you never touch the stuff. Bloody miracle, that is.'

Tony was looking at Baldock with respect, maybe even affection. He was glad to be the number one runner, to have moved up from the ranks. He was glad to be in the same room as Baldock, even if the boss still lived in a terrace. The boys had talked about that a lot. Christ, Tone, they said, he must be loaded by now, why's he still here? You lot got shit for brains, Tony would answer. Baldock is clever, see. 'E's not gonna flaunt it, is he? Nah, he'll 'ave it stashed somewhere. I wouldn't be surprised if 'e 'as a place in Spain already. Like them London gangsters.'

'Off you go, then, Smart Tony.'

Tony grinned his gap-toothed smile and twirled around.

'Like my new jacket, boss? I'm on a promise tonight. Bird called Mandy. She looks a bit like Karen only no' so classy, and she's ...'

Tony stopped suddenly.

'Christ, sorry, boss. I shouldn't have mentioned her.'

Baldock pointed to the door.

'I'll be off then.'

Tony went swiftly and gladly, making Baldock smile for the second time that day. Power always gave him a buzz. Tony had put Karen into Baldock's mind. His one failure. Karen would have made things complete if she'd stayed. He saw her that first time, when he'd been to check on Tony, the runner he could trust most. Karen was Tony's cousin who just happened to be staying there. She'd been coming down the stairs with a towel on her wet hair, looking at him with eyes that said they knew everything, eyes so blue they startled him. She wore a thin strip of skirt that almost started and ended at her belly button, and a pink T-shirt that told him instantly that she was not wearing a bra. Karen had met his eyes with confidence, standing halfway up the stairs with one hand on the towel and the other on her hip. She was tall, for a valley girl; her legs seemed to go on for ever and Baldock was impressed. For a moment he'd lost his cool, flicking back his hair nervously, before he remembered he was The Man, and that Tony was watching. Tony had grinned like the fool he was and introduced Karen like she was a trophy to be offered to Baldock. He'd accepted.

Baldock had another image, Karen coming out of the shower that first time she stayed the night. Perfect body, jet black hair, china blue dolls' eyes staring at him under her fringe. Pulling him onto the bed like she was in charge. She was that time. Clambering all over him like an animal, biting his ear, biting him all over, quickly working her way down ...

The old man was knocking the floor above him. He kept an old miner's boot just for this. There were repeated thumps on the floorboards.

'Alright!' Baldock shouted. 'Keep your hair on, what you got left of it!'

He put the teapot on a tray and added a few biscuits. His father was a stubborn old sod, like he was a stubborn young one, and he always insisted on a teapot. The old man was just about able to stomach tea bags but not if they were in a mug. Tea had to be poured, he said, the way your mother made it. She'd been dead more than ten years now, just before Baldock started dealing hash – just as well, probably.

Baldock had an older sister somewhere, Emma, but she hadn't bothered with him or their father for years. He wasn't even sure where she lived now. Emma was a looker, and had married some middle-class ponce. Some sort of property developer rip-off merchant she saw as her ticket out. She bought that ticket. Baldock hadn't seen her for years but knew she had a few kids now and was living down on the coast. She was depriving the old man of his grandchildren and he hated her for that.

When he got to forty Baldock planned to retire from dealing and invest in something legit. Something he could really make a fortune from. Then he'd find out where Emma was and go down there, maybe in an Aston Martin – no, too many poxy soccer players drove *them*. Perhaps something Italian and rare. A Ferrari from the sixties in gleaming red. He'd have BB1 on the plate – Baldock Bond. From what the doc had said his father wouldn't be around by then. His chest was shot with coal dust and they were still waiting for the compensation money. It was difficult to stop the old man getting worked up about this, when Baldock knew that a few grand was nothing to himself. He couldn't tell the old man this though, because his father had no idea of Baldock's secret world or the stash of money he'd made from it. The fact he'd taken to his bed years ago made this easier.

Baldock was a cash man, strictly cash. And it was all in the house, there was no other place for it. He stashed it in a big wooden box he'd used for toys when he was a kid, the notes hidden in a secret bottom section that he'd created himself. He'd take out the money and count it every so often, late at night, when the old man was asleep, and most of the village with him. This was like a ritual. He liked the feel of the notes – all twenties. He'd run them through his hands, put them into small stacks, even smell the buggers. They were his friends, the only things he really trusted. Then he'd put the total in the small accounts book that stayed with the notes. There was over a hundred grand now, well over. It was amazing how it had built up. Like the old coal spoils outside the window, going up higher and higher when he was a kid, as sure as night follows day. People round here smoked a lot of spliffs. This was Baldock's security, his escape money, his reason for living. After Karen went he told himself this more and more. Get out at forty. Get away. Somewhere hot, where he could be cool.

Chapter Two

Baldock took the tray upstairs, before the old man could knock again. The television was on with no sound.

'Look at this lot. Boxers be buggered. More like two dancing bears. Too fat and too thick, the pair of them.'

'That's how it is now, Dad.'

'Aye – *now*. Christ, I used to come up from a shift and box in the bloody night when I started.'

The old man's chest rippled and he went into a bout of coughing, a series of rasps, as if his lungs were trying to tear themselves away from the dust. Baldock stood by the bed patiently with his tray, not showing much concern. Neither man liked showing pity.

The old man sucked in more air.

'Aye, straight off a shift, for five bloody pound.'

'Here's your tea,' Baldock said. 'Don't tip it over the bed.'

'Thanks, son. Did I hear someone downstairs just now?'

'Only Tony.'

'I hope he's more useful than his old man. Sick note bloody Jones, we used to call 'im. The closest he usually got to coal was when he sat in front of the fire.'

Baldock's father was in good form today. The type of form when nothing was left unsaid. The old man thought speaking your mind, no matter how much you pissed someone off, was healthy, and honest. Sometimes Baldock thought it was his father's way of keeping going.

Baldock stood by the window, letting the afternoon sunshine warm his back. He watched his father slurp his tea, thinning grey hair slicked back over his head in defiant strands – the old man still had a bit of vanity in him. His watery blue eyes were still active. They were the same colour as his old mining scars, but Baldock's eyes were brown, like his mother. She'd died of cancer as soon as his father had retired, as if she couldn't face his moaning any longer. His sister had gone by then and Baldock had thought of getting away himself, but he had been busy getting his empire together. Thinking back now, he realised he had nowhere to go anyway.

His father turned off the TV.

'Waste of time,' he muttered, 'all of it.'

'Have you read the paper? It's kicking off in Iraq.'

'There's always been trouble in the world. Always will be. I don't need a paper to tell me that.'

'You're in a great mood today.'

'Well, you're getting on my nerves. Always around the house.'

'I'm supposed to be around the house. I'm your carer, remember. That's what I get paid for.'

'Not much of a job for a man.'

'Would you rather some strange woman here, looking after you?'

That shut the old man up.

It was true, Baldock was a carer, and the state paid him for it. The old man was perfect cover, especially now when things had got tricky with TJ. He should have seen that coming. The kid had built up a habit, he was into every illegal drug he could get his hands on. He'd always been the one most likely to stray. And now he thought he could branch out into Baldock's territory. The kid had almost fouled up a smooth operation, and had been skimming off the top for months. Baldock's mobile rang. It was Tony.

'TJ's been seen,' Tony said. 'The stupid sod's back with his mother, can you believe that? Rob saw him sneaking in the back way last night.'

'Okay. Go on about your business and leave him alone.'

Baldock's father snorted, nodding at the mobile.

'Isn't the phone downstairs enough for you?'

Baldock sighed. 'Want me to get you one, Dad?'

'Now who the hell would I phone, you soft bugger.'

Booking your place in heaven might be good, Baldock thought to himself. He grinned at the thought of the old man up there, shouting the odds at St Pete.

'What's so funny?'

'Do you feel like going downstairs, Dad? We hardly ever use that stairlift.'

'Nah. Pass me that boxing book.'

It was a thick volume on long-gone fighters that his father had almost worn out with his shuffling fingers. It was the closest thing to a bible he had.

'I'm going out for a while,' Baldock said. 'Be alright?'

'Aye, go on, you. Give me a bit of peace.'

Baldock often left his father when business called, and it was certainly calling tonight. He locked up – locking in the old man was the safest way – and left their large end-terrace by the back door. He'd sit on the hillside for an hour, until the light faded. Darkness was best for what he had in mind. TJ wasn't going anywhere tonight, though Baldock was surprised he'd gone back home. Then he thought some more about it and realised that TJ must have tried to run but found he had nowhere to run to, and now had nowhere to hide. So he'd gone back to his mammy, where he'd try to keep his head down and hope all his troubles would go away. Like an ostrich that sticks its head in the sand.

Baldock sat on an outcrop of rock above the terraces, where he had played as a kid, and lit a cigarette. He was trying to give up the fags, but it was hard. He had a sense of calm as he sucked in deeply, looking down on the rows of terraces curving along the valley floor. Looking down on his world. This was how he liked to think of it, Baldock's World, Baldock's Kingdom – yes, he did think of himself as a kind of monarch. In the hazy, soft yellow light of summer dusk he could see the remains of former glories that lay scattered around the valley. The mounds of old pit spoils that had been greened over but did not fit into the landscape, and, in the distance, a solitary pithead that had been left standing as a reminder of old times. They were trying to attract tourists to the valley now but Baldock hadn't seen any,

Baldock remembered TJ's mother from school. Julie had been cute at fifteen, wearing badly by twenty, old at thirty. His father was right. Time *was* passing. Baldock would definitely get out at forty. His caring would probably be over by then, and he would have enough in the stash. He'd led a charmed life. The police had seemed oblivious to him, when others had gone down. He seemed untouchable.

Something swooped low overhead. It was a hawk. It hadn't expected Baldock to be on the rock and was startled when Baldock moved. It sped away, showing its light brown belly, which the last of the light caught. Baldock envied it; he'd always envied birds of prey. They led short, savage lives, but lives that were totally free. Baldock got up and stretched. It was time to pay TJ a visit.

Chapter Three

Despite his size – he was well built, and over six feet tall – Baldock moved quickly and surely over the ground and came into TJ's estate from the hillside, well away from the main road. He hadn't been here for a long time. Others did the work for him now. If the place had changed, it was for the worse. He skirted gardens full of junk and rubbish, like adventure playgrounds for the insane. Baldock glanced back to the mountain to see a last smear of light strike the trees, a moment of green colour fade to black. It was just about dark now, how he liked it.

TJ's house was in a dead-end street. One window was boarded up, another marked by a net curtain lank with dirt. A kid's trike in need of a wheel lay on the front path. Baldock went round the back and stood for a moment outside the door. He heard raised voices. One of them was TJ's. He followed the argument. TJ's mother wanted him gone. 'You bring nothing but trouble to the house!' she yelled. Too late, mate, Baldock whispered to himself.

Baldock kicked open the door. It wasn't hard – the door was thin wood starting to rot. It fell apart under his heavy boot. TJ was sitting at a small kitchen table, rolling a smoke. His face drained of what colour it had.

'Jesus Christ! Baldock! Look, I can explain, mun.'

As if she'd been programmed, TJ's mother started to scream and shout, a wicked combination she thought might have an effect on Baldock. As she stood in front of him TJ jumped up, trying to get away. It was hopeless. Baldock caught him with a large hand and flung him against a wall. TJ was no weight at all. He sank down, dazed.

'Leave him alone, Baldock. He ain't done nothing.'

'You know better than that, love. Julie, isn't it? Long time no see.'

Despite her rage, Julie dabbed at her hair.

'Don't hurt him, Baldock. He didn't know what he was doing. He never does when he's on the hard stuff.'

TJ nodded agreement from the floor, where he sat rubbing his head. Baldock thought the scene quite funny but didn't show it. TJ had been a bloody fool and Baldock did not want to deal with this stuff any more.

'Relax,' Baldock said. 'TJ, get your arse in that chair and don't move. I'll break your legs if you do.'

'Sure boss. Okay.'

'So, it's boss again, is it?'

TJ sat down. Baldock saw that he was shaking. A skinny runt in a dirty T-shirt, nine stone soaking wet.

'So, how much did you take altogether?' Baldock said quietly.

'I dunno, boss. It all went on stuff down the valley.'

'I've worked it out – about a grand, I'd say. So, stealing from me *and* using other dealers ... not good, TJ.'

'He didn't know what he was doing,' TJ's mother said.

'Yeah, no one ever does, and you've told me that already.'

The mother had changed moods now. She was pleading with Baldock. She'll change instantly, Baldock thought, try anything. Blood was thicker than water. Even TJ's. Baldock took out his wallet and counted out five twenties. He put them on the table in a fan shape.

'I'm a reasonable man,' he said. 'Everything's cool. I'm not going to touch him, just want to get a few things straight, that's all.'

TJ looked at the money in amazement. He hadn't expected anything like this. It made him even more scared.

'This is to keep your mouth shut,' Baldock said. 'Don't worry about the door, the council will fix that. I'm going to take TJ with me. We need to get a few things straight.'

'Gimme something, Baldock,' TJ pleaded. 'I gotta score soon or I'll go crazy.'

'All in good time. By the way, why'd you come back, TJ?'

'Didn' 'ave nowhere to go, did I? Look, I'll work for nothing now. I did a good job until ...'

'It's the *until* that bothers me.'

Baldock got up and dragged TJ to his feet. His mother sat holding the money, torn between need and loyalty. Baldock pushed TJ in front of him, and the boy made no attempt to get away. He staggered towards the door like a drunken man. Baldock knew any act of kindness now would be seen as an act of weakness and Baldock wasn't known for weakness. He couldn't afford to be.

'Where we going?' TJ whimpered. 'I don' wanna go nowhere, Baldock.'

'Stop snivelling.'

Turning his back on the mother was a mistake. One Baldock would never have made

21

a few years ago. He'd been spending too much time with the old man since Karen left. It had tuned down his instincts.

For Julie, loyalty won against need.

She snatched up a kettle and hit Baldock on the back of the head with it. She was just about able to reach. He'd had far worse but it was enough to knock him down. He made a grab at TJ as he fell, but the kid was gone, bolting through the door like the scared animal he was.

'Run, TJ, run!' his mother shouted.

Baldock got up quickly and again felt the need to smile. TJ's mother had backed against the wall, five feet one of fear and defiance. Baldock chuckled.

'Bloody hell, Julie, you got more balls than that son of yours. You were like that in school, as I remember.'

'I'm surprised you bloody do, big shot like you.'

A kid was crying upstairs.

'You've woke up Damien now.'

'Where's his father?'

'Buggered off.'

Julie's eyes strayed to the money on the table but she did not reach for it. Baldock picked it up and thought of putting it back in his wallet.

'Here you are. I must be mad, giving this to someone who just tried to batter me. No *man* has for a long, long time.'

Baldock felt the back of his head. It was wet. He wiped it in one of the twenties, making a red smear. 'Now that's what I call *blood* money. It's hush money, too, Julie. I'll take this bump on the head if you keep your mouth shut. You know I'm going to catch up with TJ, so keep quiet and you'll get him back. Talk and you'll get him back in pieces.'

Julie snatched up the money.

'I gotta see to the kid,' she said.

Outside in TJ's garden Baldock shut his eyes and cursed. He couldn't believe he'd let the little git get away. It would be all over the village in a day. At least all over his world. TJ would get cheap cider off one of his scabby mates and start bragging. Baldock sighed and looked up at the stars and wished they would beam him up. They were showing strongly tonight, for some of the street lights on TJ's road were broken. Hard white points twinkled down on him, not caring a jot about him or anyone else on his sad planet. Baldock had been interested in stuff like this once, how the universe worked, but it blew his head away. He could not grasp the size of everything and gave up trying.

TJ would have to wait for another day.

Chapter Four

The old man was asleep when Baldock got back and he gave thanks for this small mercy. Sleepless nights were usual for him. He cleared up the tea tray in the bedroom, going through suitable punishments for TJ in his mind. The old man had fallen asleep with one of his old photo albums open on the bed. There was one of him in the last big war, standing proudly by his tank. Baldock swore his father thought his wartime experiences were the best thing that had ever happened to him.

Gently, Baldock took the book from his father's hands and looked through it himself. It was familiar territory for him, too, now. When his mother had been alive, the scrapbook was rarely seen. Most of the photos were black and white, many yellowing at the edges. His father was fit and powerfully built then, always ready to show off his torso to his mates. He'd been the army middleweight champion and had survived the war with just the one wound, despite being on many battlefields. As Baldock turned the worn pages he realised he was quite proud of the old man. He'd not asked anyone for anything in his life, and took no nonsense from anyone, either. A good way to be, Baldock thought.

Baldock tidied up the bed, put the light off and went downstairs before he remembered about his head. He checked it in the bathroom mirror. It was just a graze. Sticking his head under the cold water tap washed away the small patch of blood and there was no further bleeding. He smiled at his reflection in the mirror, a sheepish smile when he thought how he'd let that Julie get the better of him. It was that mother thing again. He'd seen it so many times. Blind protective love, no matter how little their offspring deserved it.

Baldock decided to check out his money stash, as he often did when things were going wrong, and TJ had gone badly wrong. The notes calmed him. Money had become so important to him that sometimes he thought it was better than sex. But only if he kept Karen out of his head. He hated the effect she still had on him, though he liked it too, if he was honest. There had been many before her, too many, but no one since.

Baldock closed the blinds, got out the money box and started to arrange the twenties in columns. It was almost like a kid's game. He felt himself calming as he fondled the notes. They were symbols of his success, the result of it. He was planning a trip to Switzerland soon, if he could get someone to look after the old man. He needed to deposit the money in a safer place than the house. Also, they might decide to bring in a new twenty pound note. He knew a few other dealers who had been caught out like that the last time. They had to rush out and buy a Merc or a house, or both. Drawing the police to them for sure.

Baldock sat back, lit a cigarette and looked at his money like a proud father. He took a deep drag on his smoke and sent grey smoke around the room to mingle with the blue. He enjoyed everything about smoking, but he planned to give it up as soon as he stopped dealing. Baldock wanted to enjoy his new life as long as possible.

It was starting to rain. Baldock heard it on the flat roof of the house extension. It didn't take long to get going. Within a minute it was belting down. He loved the rain, the way it cleansed everything. He sat back in his father's old armchair and watched it through the front window. He was almost nodding off when his mobile rang. He became alert quickly, spilling cigarette ash on himself.

'Hello?'

There was a moment's silence but Baldock heard the intake of breath on the other side.

'Is that you, TJ, you little weasel?'

'No, it's not one of your scummy friends.'

Karen. He almost dropped the phone.

'Well, say something, then. Not often you're lost for words.'

'No.'

'Well, what you doing, then?'

'You're something else, Karen. You walk out on me six months ago and phone me up to ask me something like that. Don't tell me you're having a kid.'

Karen was a great shrugger and he could see her doing it now. The shrug of the shoulders and toss of the hair. Like she'd been on that first date, wearing that come-and-get-me dress. All confidence and cheek. And something else. Something that had sunk a hook in his gut. It was there now, and he could feel it tugging.

'Don't be stupid. Are you on your own?' Karen asked. 'Not counting your father. How is he, by the way?'

'As ever, and yes, there's no woman here, if that's what you mean.'

'Good, because I'm outside the back door.'

Baldock had his second shock in a minute.

'Lemme in, then. I don't want to wake your father.'

Chapter Five

Baldock's neat columns of notes were quickly put back in their box in grabbed handfuls. He winced at the untidiness, almost feeling as if he was abusing the money. He put the box in a cupboard and opened the back door. Karen walked into the light. He wondered if she was about to walk into his life again, but told himself this couldn't happen. It wouldn't happen. His pride wouldn't allow it. Karen slouched past him looking a million dollars.

'Took your time, didn't you,' Karen said. 'You look older, bits of grey in your hair. Must be all that ducking and diving.'

'What do you want, Karen?'

'Got any drink here?'

For Baldock, this was almost too much, coming so soon after his TJ experience. He didn't know whether to throw her out, maybe even give her a slap. Not that he'd ever hit her in the past. Anger flared up in him. It very rarely got the better of him now, but in the past it had been his worst enemy. All those sayings like *red mist* and *lost control* had meaning for him. There'd been many times when his fists would bunch up and he just wanted to lash out. It had started early, in junior school, and by the time he finished what little education he'd had, local people knew Baldock as someone to be feared. It had made it much easier to create his dealing world.

'Well?'

'Well what?'

'Have you got something to bloody drink, or not?'

Baldock breathed deeply and was in control again.

'There's a few bottles of lager in the fridge.'

'Let's have one, then.'

Baldock opened two bottles and handed one to Karen. He waved his hand towards the sofa and sat back down on his armchair. He did not trust himself to get too close to Karen but his eyes didn't leave her. Her hair was different, much lighter, almost a dirty blond, and she'd lost a few pounds, but still had the looks that would make male tongues dangle in the local pubs. She wore a leather jacket loosely over her shoulders and tight jeans that looked like an extra skin.

'How'd you get here,' Baldock asked, 'at this time at night?'

'Got a motor now. A new Mini.'

'You're not on the game, are you?'

'Cheeky bastard. I'm modelling – proper modelling. I told you I could – and would.'

Baldock remembered it well. Their last row, when Karen said she wanted to earn real money, not the peanuts she got in the local hairdressers. He'd laughed. She wanted him to get out of dealing, too. Get a real job. What other people did, not Baldock.

'Some guy came onto me in a bar,' Karen said. 'I thought he was just tossing me a line when he went on about modelling. But it turned out that Karl was gay, and his offer was for real. He got me into an agency and things went from there. It took off quick. I'm a natural, they say, whatever that means. Karl is talking about London now. He's got loads of contacts.'

'That's nice for him. So, why are you here? It's almost midnight, for God's sake.'

'Well, you never liked ordinary women, did you, Baldock? At least you said you didn't.'

Baldock's head was in a mess. The six months since he'd seen Karen had dripped away slowly. He'd busied himself by trying to up his profits, and looking after the old man. They'd become an odd couple, but it worked, in a way. His father would try Baldock's patience to the limit, then pull back. It had become a kind of game Baldock didn't mind playing. He'd never had a problem with the old man. He realised now that he should never have grown up like he had. Most of the other dealers, and their customers, had a raft of problems. He couldn't think of one who'd had two parents at the same time but Baldock's early life had been steady, his parents always there for him. The dealing had just happened, like most things in life.

Karen took a pull at her opened bottle.

'Just as talky as ever, I see,' she muttered. 'Don't know what to say, do you. You never did like surprises.'

Baldock took a long swallow from his own bottle as Karen spread herself over the sofa. He told himself to play it cool but he was already undressing her with his eyes.

'So, got your hook into anyone, then?' Baldock asked.

'Now and then. No one special. You?'

Baldock shrugged. 'I'm not bothered.'

'Don't know why not. This place is full of slappers who think you're God.'

'Not interested.'

'No, you weren't with me, much. Only when you thought I might go.'

'You did.'

'I think Baldock is the centre of Baldock's universe.'

'Nothing wrong with that.'

'No, not if you're a control freak who's like a bloody icicle.'

'Did you come here to have a fight? Or do you want to score? Is that it?'

'I'm not one of your losers. I never was.'

Baldock got up and walked around the room. He drained his lager and wasn't sure why he was drinking it. He'd never liked it much. Now its coldness hit the back of his head, reminding him of his earlier failure.

'What's this about TJ?' Karen asked.

'What the hell do you know about that?'

'You know what the grapevine's like. Julie's okay. She helped me out a few times when I was a kid. I used to go round there when mum had a new *uncle* on the go ... I had a lot of uncles, never a father.'

'She hasn't sent you round here, has she?'

Baldock cursed himself again. If he'd kept hold of TJ, all of this would be done and dusted. Karen was right about the control thing. He hated things going wrong, hated surprises, anything that affected the smooth operation of Baldock's world. Karen had

34

affected it before, and it looked as if she wanted to do so again.

Baldock sat down on the sofa, pushing her legs away.

'Why'd you change your hair? I liked it black.'

She kissed him quickly, before he could push her away. It was more a bite. He felt her sharp teeth dig at his lips but did nothing. He knew he should throw her out. Karen might be up to anything. Then she kissed him again and all such thoughts left his mind.

Chapter Six

For an hour, Karen assaulted Baldock. He thought of it like that. An assault. She was all over him. Pulling at his shirt, ripping off his jeans, using her mouth like a killer weapon. Small, sharp bite-kisses worked their patterns around him. It took him a while to respond, but he did. Fighting her to see who would stay on top. At some point Baldock thought he heard the old man knocking again, but the sound was lost in the actions of their sweating, over-worked bodies.

'Forget how good it was, didn't you,' Karen gasped.

'Shut up, you bitch,' Baldock whispered as he lost all control.

Baldock could feel Karen's heart still working overtime as she lay on his chest.

'Your muscle tone is going,' she whispered. 'You used to have a great six pack. Now it's turning flabby.'

'That's not what you said just now.'

'Where's your fags? I'm gasping.'

'On the table.'

Karen reached over to grasp the packet. She was almost thirty now, but still had a young girl's breasts, small and firm, her pert nipples still aroused. Baldock had been right about the old man. He was knocking again, and there was a faint shout to go with it.

Karen giggled.

'We must have woke him up. He probably thinks you're having a fit,' she whispered.

'You never used to make such a noise.'

Karen giggled again.

'Better go up and see to the old bugger.'

Baldock dressed quickly, checked his face for any marks, and went upstairs.

The old man was sitting up in bed with the bedside light on.

'Took your bloody time, didn't you.'

'Sorry. I nodded off.'

'Aye, with the telly on. What the hell are you watching, anyway?'

'Nothing. It was just on.'

His father looked at him suspiciously but Baldock doubted that he could ever guess the truth. The old man had liked Karen, thought he might have been gaining a daughter when things were going good.

'Can't sleep,' the old man muttered. 'Aches all over, I got.'

'It's all those old fights coming back to haunt you.'

'Aye, maybe. Lots of things come back to haunt you when you're my age.'

'Do you want another pot of tea?'

'Nah. Open those blinds.'

'What for?'

'I want to look out the window. What else would I want to open them for?'

'Well, there won't be much to see.'

Baldock did as he was told. Orange street light flooded into the room.

'These new lights are too bright, mun. Like searchlights, they are. Seems like everyone's afraid of the dark nowadays.'

'It's all the scallies, Dad. They got people running scared.'

'Bah. There's never any real trouble around here. Never will be. It's getting like this country's afraid of its own shadow. They got cameras all over the place, too.'

'Yip.'

The old man settled down again and Baldock closed his own eyes for a moment. He was thinking of TJ, and the woman downstairs. He needed to assess the situation quickly. Karen was a woman on a mission, that was obvious, and she'd paved the way with her body. His heart was still pounding, and his head wasn't that clear, either. It was starting to throb a little. Maybe Julie's kettle strike had done more damage than he thought.

The old man fell asleep again. Baldock heard his father's uneven breathing as his lungs, or what was left of them, fought against the dust. It was a rasping, rhythmical sound, quite high pitched, like an old-fashioned singing kettle about to boil. Baldock had grown up with it. His father had breathed like this for as long as he could remember. It was almost comforting now. One of the constants of his life. As his father grew more difficult and grumpy Baldock often wished that the end would come, but he dreaded it too. A strange bond had grown up between them since his mother had died. Baldock wondered how his father would react if he knew about his son's secret world. He did not want to think about it. Quietly, Baldock made his way back downstairs.

Chapter Seven

Karen had also dressed. She lay back on the sofa, smoking another of Baldock's cigarettes.

'Is he alright?' she asked. 'He didn't hear us, did he?'

'Hear you, you mean. No, he thought I had the telly on.'

Karen smiled, and wrapped her lips around her smoke, like she'd wrapped her lips around Baldock. She always did things in the most personal way. Baldock sat back in his armchair and finished the rest of his bottle of lager. It tasted flat.

'So, what exactly do you know about TJ?' Baldock asked.

'I know he's stitched you up. Been skimming off the top, hasn't he? I'm surprised the little bugger had the nerve.'

'He's got onto the hard stuff. He's a smackhead now.'

'Yeah, I know. Julie said. He's just feeding the habit. She blames you.'

'Aye, she would. Anyone but TJ and herself. But you know I only do dope. That's nothing.

Booze and those' – Baldock pointed to Karen's cigarette – 'are much worse.'

'Maybe.'

'TJ would have got onto it anyway, with or without me. He was the type.'

'What type is that?'

'The hopeless type. The type that's got to put something into their lives, something to fill up the nothing. Something to get them up in the morning, or the afternoon, in TJ's case.'

'What are you going to do, then?'

'I'm not sure, yet.'

'Oh yes, you are. You're going to hurt him, aren't you?'

'I can't let it go. Don't worry, he'll live.'

'You think you're so big, Baldock. Mister bloody big and his slaves.'

'The man you were all over, just now.'

Karen threw the remnants of his cigarette at him. Baldock blocked it with his hand and was showered in sparks.

'Temper, temper. Is that what really brought you back here, Karen? TJ bloody Davies?'

Karen ran her hand through her long hair, tossing it around. Baldock tensed for an attack but she calmed down. Something she'd never been able to do so quickly before.

'How long is it going to go on, then?'

'What?'

'Your bloody dealing.'

'Not sure.'

Baldock was sure. He'd made a firm decision to end it. At forty.

'You never did explain why you finished us,' Baldock murmured. 'Not really.'

'I didn't want to end up one of your slaves.'

'When we started you earned nothing in that hairdressers. I showed you another life.'

'You're not going to take the credit for my modelling, are you?'

'Maybe.'

'God, you're an arrogant bastard. I'm having another lager. You want one?'

'No.'

Karen's long legs whisked past Baldock's face. He wanted her again, but would not show it. Karen came back with the bottle in her hand, and stood behind him. He could hear her swallow slowly.

'Is that why you're here, Karen? To plead for TJ? That's pretty weird, if you are.'

'I might get out of the valley for good,' Karen said, leaving the question unanswered. 'I'll be thirty soon. Bloody thirty.'

'So?'

'I want to do something better with my life.

This is a place of dead-ends, and dead-heads.'

'I've made it work for me.'

'Yeah, by taking the chance of being banged up for five years – or more.'

'That'll never happen.'

'That's what they all say. Look, why not let TJ go? He's never going to do anything like that again.'

'No, he's never going to get the chance. Look, you know how it is round here. TJ has crossed me. If I let it go, what kind of signal am I sending out? They'll say Baldock has gone soft, and they'll all be ripping me off.'

'You could stop. You must have enough money. And I'm earning good, now.'

'And we'd start up again, is that what you're saying? All this for that little runt. Not very romantic.'

Karen raised her voice.

'Of course it's not just for him, but when Julie phoned me it got me to thinking about us, about how it hadn't been too bad – most of the time.'

'Keep your voice down, or the old man will be knocking again. It was more than not bad just now.'

Karen grinned. 'I know and I got a flat now. A few miles down the valley.'

'You know I can't leave the old man.'

'It's not going to be for much longer, is it?'

'Hard to tell.'

'Well, do you fancy it, or what?'

Baldock got up and took hold of Karen.

'I fancy this.'

This time he was in charge. His brain had recovered from the shocks forced on it and he did not flinch as Karen ran her hands over his head, pressing down on the kettle wound. Maybe he *could* start again with Karen. He'd be lying if he said he hadn't missed her. But TJ was something else. TJ was business.

Chapter Eight

It was getting on for three in the morning when Karen left. Baldock watched her go in her metallic blue Mini. She had K100 on the back plate, beating him to BB1. He stayed on the front porch for a while, smoking a last cigarette and enjoying the soft rain on his face. He looked out on the night world of the village, silent, and slicked by the rain, lit by the hard orange street lights. The old man was right, it seemed like it was never truly dark any more, unless you got far up on the hillside.

Baldock used to walk the hillsides a lot at night, before his father needed so much care. He liked the stillness and the peace. He was a night owl who liked to walk around with just the moon and stars for company, and prided himself on knowing every inch of his land, day or night. He wondered if TJ was up there now. Shivering and scared like a wild animal on the run, unable to go back to his feisty mother, unable to go anywhere. His body crying out for its next fix. Tomorrow Baldock would go looking. It wouldn't take long to find TJ, now he'd been flushed out.

It was ten o'clock in the morning. Baldock's father had been fed and taken to the bathroom. He could manage in there on his own but Baldock had to stay close. The DSS had given them a wheelchair, but the old man hated it.

'I'm not being seen in that thing,' he'd shouted, when Baldock first showed it to him. 'Like some old woman in a chariot.'

Baldock had managed to get him out in it once, feeling as self-conscious as a young father pushing a pram. The old man had grunted his way around the village, giving instructions like the tank driver he'd once been, a teenager in the war he rarely talked about.

Baldock began his work-out routine. Karen had spurred him into action. He had a makeshift gym in the shed at the back of the house where he pumped iron, did fifty press-ups each morning, and punished his body for an hour most days. He didn't feel right if he missed a session but Karen was right. It was getting harder to stop muscle going soft. Baldock needed to work that girl out of his system, at least for a while.

As he raised the weights above his head he thought of TJ. He wouldn't have gone far.

Baldock planned to go looking in the late afternoon, a time when the old man was most settled. He'd take the field glasses with him and would soon spot the kid skulking about up on the hillside, working his way closer to his mother again. TJ would know how dangerous that was, but wouldn't be able to help it. He was a homing pigeon, like so many here.

Baldock finished with the press-ups. He always did. This morning he worked particularly hard, feeling the blood rushing to his brain, the strain on his arms, the wooden floor coming towards him, then going away again. He had confidence in his strength, his fitness, that had never failed him. As he showered, Baldock was aware of his body, its still taut lines and rippling muscles. He was six foot and one inch tall and fourteen stone in weight. Not too big, not too small. Perfect. He'd read somewhere that your body is a temple, and he had to admit he worshipped his.

Less than a mile away, lying under a hedge at the side of a field, TJ was having a very different experience. He'd been there all night. It had been mild but not mild enough for him, and it had rained off and on throughout the night. He was damp, crumpled, hungry, and most of all, strung out. He craved a fix. Almost enough to give himself up to Baldock, take what was coming, then get what he needed. That mainline to heaven, that place where all his troubles would go away for a while. Where he'd glide through comfortable layers and not worry about anything, until he came down. Then the world would come crashing back, in all its awful glory. And it had always been awful, for TJ. His earliest memories were of his mother being beaten, by a succession of daddies. It had been better when they were on their own, but then there'd been the penny-pinching and scraping, TJ watching the other kids in school who seemed to have everything.

When TJ started working for Baldock things began to change. Bits of money were coming in, he could help his mother more. Help himself. Then he began to see how much money was flowing to Baldock, which made his own few quid look so small. When he met that girl temptation began to fight against fear and gradually temptation won. It seemed so easy at first, an extra twenty for himself here and there. Then thirty, forty, until it became blatant. He knew he'd be caught out but couldn't stop. Now it was over and he'd have to pay. TJ was afraid but also understanding. He'd gone against the hand that had fed him and that was wrong. Almost as bad as grassing someone up. If Baldock didn't do anything Tony and the other runners would. It *would* be Baldock though, especially after last night. TJ couldn't believe Julie had done that. Stupid cow. His mother had made things worse.

TJ rolled over on the lumpy ground and managed to find a crushed packet of fags in his pocket but no lighter. It must have dropped out somewhere when he ran. Bastard! He muttered this to himself over and over. But at least the sun was coming out. He sat with his knees hunched up, facing the sun, letting it dry his clothes. He was resigned to being caught by Baldock, but knew he would also try to run when it came to it. It was instinct.

It was mid-afternoon. Baldock had about six hours of daylight and dusk left. He expected to find TJ before it got dark. This was the way he wanted to time it, so that any punishment might be carried out as darkness came on. The old man had been good today, and had kept his moaning to a minimum. It was one of his father's mellow days, and they were getting few and far between.

'I'll be popping out in a while, Dad,' Baldock said, standing by his father's bedroom window.

'What for?'

'Just a bit of business.'

'Aye, monkey business. You're paid to stay here with me.'

'You'll be alright for a few hours.'

'Well, I'll have to be, won't I?'

'You've had your food, been to the bog. You want anything else before I go?'

'Nah, you get off on your *business*.'

Baldock went into his own bedroom to prepare himself. It was a sparse room, a bed and not much furniture. Even as a kid Baldock hadn't been much interested in music, even less so in books, although his father always had his head in one. Books about the 'old days'. The old man would utter this phrase like it was some sort of magic spell, some never-never land that was so much better than now. If Baldock could have had a pound for every time his father said 'we didn't have much in those days but we were happy' there would have been no need to start his empire.

Baldock dressed in his mountain combat gear. Green camouflage jacket, matching trousers and Doc Martin high lace-up boots. He had a powerful pair of binoculars he'd taken instead of money once from one of the boys. It had probably been knocked off in a burglary. He'd had time to examine his head now, using two mirrors. It was just a graze, and was already drying up. Just as well Julie hadn't used something more solid.

Baldock was ready to go when the old man shouted for him.

'What?'

Baldock went back up to him.

'I can't find my lighter for my roll-ups.'

'You shouldn't be smoking, anyway.'

'Don't start that again. If I'd known I'd live this long maybe I would have looked after myself a bit more, but it's too bloody late now.'

'Here it is. Under one of your pillows.'

Baldock put the lighter in the bedside cabinet alongside the bed.

'Now don't lose it again. Look, you got your panic button. You should be wearing it around your neck. Press it and my mobile will ring, and for God's sake, Dad, don't press it by accident – it'll also ring the emergency services. For a moment Baldock imagined police going through the house, some wide-eyed young pig coming across his stash.

'Alright, alright. I'm not senile, not yet.'

Baldock smiled.

'You'll never be that, Dad.'

The old man looked his son up and down.

'Christ, you look like a German soldier.'

'It's comfortable gear. Be back soon.'

Chapter Nine

Before he left Baldock got his money from its hiding place. He counted out five hundred pounds, then another five hundred as an afterthought and put the money into his old leather wallet. The wallet had been a present from his parents when he got to eighteen, and it had served him well down the years. Then Baldock did something he'd never done. He went to the black tin and got out a few dope wraps. He hadn't carried anything on him for years – that was for others to do. But he knew he'd need it later, when he caught up with TJ.

Baldock left the house by the back door. They had a stretch of garden that led onto the hillside through a wooden gate, and Baldock took this route. He had a natural instinct to avoid prying eyes, and there were many of these in the village.

He made ground quickly, sure-footed with long strides until he got to his favourite spot, the outcrop of rock that gave him a perfect view of the widest expanse of hillside. Using the glasses he could see TJ's rancid estate, his own terrace, and all the land between. It was mainly rough fields and hedgerows dotted with sheep and a few horses. Farmers had cut back most of the bracken years ago, which made Baldock's job much easier.

He sat with the rock against his back, out of the keen wind, and slowly began to track the glasses back and forth across the hillside. TJ would be on the edge of despair now, hacked off, frightened and wanting shelter. Like all animals on the run.

Thoughts raced through Baldock's head. They always did, but today he was on overdrive. Karen was centre stage and he couldn't get her off. What she was offering was a form of blackmail and Baldock would never put up with that, but last night had been good. Sex had always been good with Karen, often wild and unexpected. She was a girl who loved to take chances. It was the other stuff that had finished them. She'd started to use the *commitment* word, which had frightened him. He could manage it with the old man, he was family, and had always been there, but the thought of living with a woman, full-time, did not appeal. At least it hadn't then. Now he wasn't so sure. Karen was right, his father wouldn't last much longer and Baldock wasn't as confident about being alone as he used to be. Concentrate on the business in hand, he told himself, even if it might blow his chances of getting back with Karen. If she put that runt TJ before him so be it. This was business and it had to be done.

Baldock stretched out his long frame and continued his sweep of the hillside. Despite the wind it was a warm day in late summer and the landscape was fat with lush growth. He saw sheep, cows, a farmer working with a tractor, a young colt playing in a field below and a man taking his dog for a walk, but no TJ. Baldock was tired. Last night had been strenuous and the old man had got him up early with his rasping shout. He put the glasses down and lit a cigarette. It would be easy to doze off in the sun as he lay back and took a long drag on his smoke, the rock behind him warm on his back.

If you kept still like this, he thought, it was amazing what you could see on the hillside. Animals forgot about you. If you didn't move you were not a threat. Only the crows veered away from him – they knew about men with guns. Baldock saw rabbits coming out for their afternoon run, and watched a pair of hawks glide near each other high up in the sky. Their flight made graceful arcs against the light clouds. Then, when he was crushing his smoke under a boot he saw TJ, scuttling along by a hedgerow. The kid looked like a scarecrow. Baldock couldn't help but chuckle. His prey was walking right towards him.

Baldock's timing was out, and he blamed Karen for it. If she hadn't been in his head, muddying everything up, he wouldn't have shown himself so soon. TJ was about thirty yards away when Baldock stood up on the rock and shouted down at him.

'TJ. Good of you to come and meet me. Nice day, innit.'

'Fuck me! Baldock!'

And TJ was gone, scurrying back down the hillside. Baldock didn't know the kid could move so fast. He got after him, trying to cut across his path before TJ could find some cover. Baldock enjoyed the chase and started to close the gap, despite being twice TJ's age.

'You're making it worse, TJ!' he shouted. 'If you stop now it will go better for you.'

TJ didn't answer. He needed all his wind and was being driven on by terror. His lungs were screaming at him to stop, and tears of despair streamed down his face. It was as if Baldock had appeared out of thin air, like some sort of magician, and he could hear Baldock closing on him. His heavy tread getting closer.

'TJ! I'm gonna fucking kill you if you don't stop!'

Cows scattered as they ran through them. One got in Baldock's way which gave TJ a few more valuable seconds. He managed to get to cover, diving into a clump of low bushes. He squirmed his way into the undergrowth and tried to hide, pushing along on his belly into the thickest part of the cover. For once, he was glad that he was so small. Baldock was only a few yards away from him. TJ could hear his heavy breathing.

'TJ, where are you?'

The bushes were thorny and almost impenetrable, unless you were pint-sized, like TJ. Baldock was getting his breath, and thinking to himself that this was proving to be hard work. There was movement at the back of the bushes. Baldock would have to go round the long way. He saw TJ break out again but could not get hold of him. He tried diving at his feet but the kid evaded his grasp, like the slippery little bugger he was. As Baldock got up something struck his face. It was a piece of turf, thrown at him in desperation by TJ.

'TJ, for fucksake! You're only putting it off, mun!'

Baldock got up and took off once more, having to close the gap between them all over again. As he did so his mobile phone spilled from his pocket and fell to the ground.

Chapter Ten

The boy had been gone for a long time. The old man felt like pressing his emergency button, just for spite. He'd gone through every channel on the telly. There were lots of them now, but mostly it was just rubbish piled on rubbish. Especially in the day. He wondered if they thought only morons watched then, or that people only put their brains in at night. He made another roll-up. It would take away the hunger he was beginning to feel. If the boy wasn't back soon he'd have to get downstairs himself. He could just about manage it on that stairlift thing they'd put in. He could use the phone there and call him on his mobile.

The old man sat propped up by pillows and enjoyed his smoke. It was a warm day and the smoke mixed with the sunlight to make patterns in the room that he thought pleasing. He watched it drift out of the open window ... smoking ... it was the only pleasure he had left.

The old man's thoughts wandered, back to the days when he was young, when his wife Mary was young, and they had it all to look forward to. He saw himself in fine shape, coal-black hair and trim figure, stepping out with the missus before the kids were born. Proud to stand out in the winter cold waiting for the colliery bus, letting the wind rip into him, whilst others packed together in the shelter. He was paying for it now, though. Riddled with arthritis as much as dust. When he tried to walk it felt like he was walking on hot coals and his hips had long given up.

His wife had been a looker, the best in the village. That was where the boy got his looks from, his mother. He shouldn't be still in the village, looking after his father. That was woman's work. He couldn't work the boy out sometimes – his son didn't seem to have any ambition. By the time he'd popped his clogs, Baldock junior might be forty plus. What would he do then?

The old man coughed, then shrugged his once powerful shoulders. He was not much of a worrier. Things would work out, or not. What people did never seemed to change things much in the end. He'd realised that long ago and driving that tank in the war had made him sure of it. One thing he *was* sure of was that he'd brought up his son to look after himself. The old man's head dropped to his chest and he fell asleep again. The half-smoked roll-up fell gently onto the floor.

Chapter Eleven

TJ was tiring. Baldock could see that by the crazy way he was running. Zig-zagging over the hillside, not knowing which way to go. Baldock tried to cut out the angles in his running, gaining on TJ steadily. The boy was running away from cover now, ever more desperate. Baldock wanted to shout out that running away made no sense but he didn't have the breath.

TJ had changed direction and was climbing again. He was getting to the top of the hillside, where the ridge dropped down steeply on the other side. Baldock knew if he got over the top he might lose him again, so he put on a final spurt. His lungs were killing him and his legs were not much better. If he felt like this, how the hell was TJ still going? The kid had been a drug free zone for days, and had probably eaten nothing since he ran from Julie's. Baldock could not understand the depth of TJ's fear because he had never known it himself.

Baldock was only yards from TJ's back now and he could hear the kid start to whimper.

Seeing his chance as TJ stumbled, Baldock made a final dive. He grabbed the back of TJ's jacket and pulled the boy down. The men lay on the hard ground, equally winded. Baldock did not even bother to hold onto TJ – the kid wasn't going anywhere. After a minute TJ got to his knees and threw up, just missing Baldock.

'Any of that goes over me and it will be even worse for you!' Baldock shouted. 'Where the hell did you think you were going, TJ? Eh?'

TJ wiped his mouth with the back of his hand.

'I don' fuckin' know, do I?'

He sat back down with a dull look on his face. Eyes glazed but still alert. Baldock wondered where he'd seen that look before. It came to him. The local cattle he'd watch as a kid, when local farmers herded them onto slaughterhouse trucks. Cows wild-eyed with fear, as if they knew what was coming, as if they could smell it and were terrified, but also resigned.

Baldock softened his voice a little.

'Relax, TJ. No one's going to die.'

Baldock sat down next to TJ, three times his size.

'What happened?' Baldock muttered. 'Did

you stop growing at twelve? How big's your father, anyway?'

'I dunno.'

'What you mean, you don't know?'

'I dunno who he was, do I. Mam said he could be one of three geezers an' I only ever seen one of them.'

Baldock took out a packet of cigarettes and offered TJ one. He grabbed it greedily and held Baldock's hand as he used his lighter. Baldock could feel the kid trembling. A shake that went all through his body. TJ sucked deeply on his smoke.

'You 'avn't got no dope on you, have you Baldock? It'll take the edge off. I'm desperate, mun.'

'Might have.'

TJ's wild eyes became wilder.

'Aw, come on, lemme score, Baldock. Look, I'll do anything to make it up to you. I'll work for nothing ... anything.'

'You'll be asking me if I got anything to eat next.'

''Ave you?'

Baldock couldn't help smiling. He took out a wrap and TJ snatched it from him. He also handed TJ the packet of cigarettes and papers and watched as TJ made up a joint. Despite his terror TJ's work was immaculate. He made roll-ups like a machine. He lit up from the cigarette he was already smoking, inhaled and lay back.

Baldock wondered if TJ thought he'd got away with it, if he was going to forgive and forget. He wanted him calm, and this was the best way. He could feel tension leaving TJ as the dope took effect.

'So, why'd you do it, TJ?'

'I got mixed up, boss. I was going out with that piece Jade – you know what she's like. Wants everything all the time, always on at me to get her things. So I started taking a bit off the top. I always planned to pay it back, I swear I did. The cow finished with me anyway – called me a loser, the bitch. By then I was in too deep.'

'You sure were.'

Chapter Twelve

TJ had packed a lot of dope into his roll-up. He floated as much as stumbled up the hillside. Once or twice Baldock had to steady him.

'Aw, 'ow much further, boss?'

'Not much.'

Baldock noticed that TJ was calling him *boss* again. The kid was trying to attach himself to Baldock once more, like a dog to its master. Maybe he thought he'd gotten away with it, that Baldock would just let him pay the money back in dribs and drabs. That would be what Karen wanted and it would be the least messy solution, but not the one Baldock wanted. He had a sudden rush of anger. All this bloody fuss over a stupid kid. He remembered when he was TJ's age, when a red mist seemed to fall on him whenever he lost his temper. Which was often. Baldock had made teenage rage into an art form, without the excuses a lot of other kids he knew could claim. He'd had two decent parents and a stable upbringing but he'd still wanted to smash everything around him. There'd been times when he had. Baldock's reputation of quick temper and even quicker fists and boots soon spread through the valley. It had never gone away.

Baldock breathed deeply, trying to control himself. Karen showing up had complicated things. Had she got the better of him last night? Was it a fifty-fifty thing? Were they getting back together – would they, after what was about to happen to TJ? Too many questions. They made his head hurt.

'Go left,' Baldock said, 'up to those rocks there.'

TJ's fear was coming back.

'What, you mean up to the Crag? Wha' we going there for?'

Baldock pushed him along.

'Just go.'

The Crag was what locals called a modest mountain-top cliff. Something had gouged out the rock long ago to make a drop of twenty feet or so from the rocky outcrop. Baldock had always sat on it when he wanted a good view of the whole valley. They got to the top.

'Why we stopping?' TJ said.

TJ sank to the ground, like he wanted to vanish into it. TJ looked like what he was, something to prey on, crouching, shivering with fear, waiting for the larger beast to fall on him. Baldock took two more wraps from his pocket and stuffed them into one of TJ's. For one blind moment TJ felt joy, until fear crushed it out again.

'Don' hurt me, boss. Please.'

'I told your mother I wouldn't touch you, and I always keep my word. You know that.'

Baldock pulled the unconvinced TJ to his feet and marched him to the edge of the cliff.

'Here's the deal, TJ. It'll be a test of faith. Do you know what faith is, TJ?'

'Nuh. I dunno what you're talking about.'

'Faith in yourself. In me. In our business.'

Baldock pushed TJ forward towards the edge of the drop. Beneath was a green carpet of ferns and undergrowth. A soft landing, or softish, anyway, Baldock thought.

'When you're ready, TJ. Pick your spot. I'm going to sit over here and enjoy the sight. I'm not going to touch you.'

'For God's sake, Baldock! You're crazy.'

'Faith, TJ. I'm offering you a way back in. Self-help, you could call it.'

'I'll bloody kill myself.'

'No, I don't think so.'

'You don't *think* so!'

TJ's face was as white as the clouds above them, his eyes wild. He stood at the edge of the cliff, frozen to the spot, like a rabbit caught in the headlights of a car.

'Don't take too long,' Baldock muttered.

Baldock took out a cigarette from his packet but dropped his lighter as he was about to use it. Maybe it was his sudden change in position as he made a grab at the lighter, maybe TJ thought Baldock was coming towards him, but suddenly TJ was gone. His cry was taken by the wind.

Baldock lit his cigarette before he got up, then walked slowly to the edge of the cliff and searched for TJ in the ferns below. He was there, moving slightly, a leg twisted under him. Baldock was impressed. He hadn't thought TJ would do it. It was just as well that he had, for Baldock did not have a plan B.

Baldock made his way down, skirting the drop, guided to TJ by his noise. He lay on the ground whimpering and it looked as if his right leg was busted but his head was alright. There wasn't a mark on his face.

Baldock crouched down and tapped TJ on the shoulder.

'See, I told you it would be alright. You've done well, my son. Come and see me when you get out of hospital. We'll wipe the slate clean now.'

'Okay.'

'And keep your mouth tight shut, TJ. You fell off the Crag, right, when you were going for a walk. Julie will try to get you to say different, but we know better, don't we?'

TJ nodded his head, and sucked in his breath with the pain. Baldock looked for his mobile. He was sure he'd brought it with him. It must dropped out of his pocket when he was running after TJ. Fuck. The boy was still causing trouble.

'Where's your mobile, TJ?'

TJ tapped a pocket, groaning as he moved when Baldock took it out. Baldock phoned for an ambulance, giving precise instructions. There was a mountain road a bit further down so they wouldn't have far to walk.

Baldock had almost forgotten about the money he was carrying. He was having second thoughts about giving it to TJ. The boy had ripped him off for enough already. Then he thought of Karen's questions later and took out his wallet. He'd hedge his bets and give TJ half. Five hundred quid would be the most the kid would have ever had in his life.

'Here you are, TJ, help take the pain away. Don't let anyone down the hospital nick it off you.'

Baldock tucked the other five hundred safe in his wallet. He'd already lost a mobile today. He stayed with TJ, who was now a mixture of resentment and relief. He helped him to roll another joint, then stood in the shadow of trees when the ambulance's siren approached. He heard TJ explain how he'd fallen whilst out for a walk and mouthed *good boy* to himself. They strapped TJ into a stretcher and took him down, taking care as the afternoon was turning to evening dusk and gloom.

Baldock checked his watch and realised he'd been away from the old man for too long. Far too long.

As he made his way down the mountain he rubbed at his eyes. He was tired, feeling his age. It really was time to spend his stash, buy a share in a club, maybe, somewhere cheap and hot.

Chapter Thirteen

Karen knocked again on Baldock's back door. She'd tried him on his mobile a few times but he wasn't answering. She wondered if he was avoiding her, if he thought last night had been a mistake, for both of them. She didn't think it was, not for her, anyway. As soon as she'd seen Baldock she knew she wanted him back.

She pressed her head against the glass panel in the door, but couldn't hear anything. But she smelt something. Smoke. She could see it drifting down Baldock's stairs. Not thick, but thick enough. Karen began to shout and kick the door, stubbing her toes inside her high heels. Baldock must be out, she thought, and he's left the old man in bed.

Karen ran out into the street, straight into Tony.

'Jesus, Karen, babe. What you doin' here? You and the boss back together?'

'Never mind that. Phone 999.'

'Huh?'

'Phone 999, you stupid sod. The house is on fire.'

'Bloody hell.'

'Get an ambulance as well.'

Karen's shouts had alerted other people. A man walking his dog crossed the road, a few others were coming out of front doors. Karen recognised the dog walker as one of the guys who used to come into the hairdressers to have his head shaved. A muscle-bound steroid-user the size of a small house. Perfect.

'Come on!' Karen shouted. 'You'll have to break the door down!'

Smoke was starting to pour from the front windows of the house. As the bodybuilder and Tony went around to the back door, Karen shouted up.

'Mr Baldock! For God's sake get up! '

She heard glass breaking. The bodybuilder had smashed through the door, Tony at his side. Karen pushed past them, and immediately the smoke hit her. It was hard to see and she began to cough. Tony held back.

'Don' go in there, love,' he said, 'it's 'opeless.'

'We gotta try!' Karen screamed. 'There's no fire. I can't see no fire!'

She pulled at the bodybuilder's arm.

'There's an old man up there!'

'Alright – I'll do it for the old man. I wouldn't for that bastard Baldock.'

The man disappeared inside. In the distance Karen heard a siren.

It was a long minute before the man reappeared. Karen heard him coughing before she saw anything. Then the bodybuilder appeared with the old man over his shoulder, crouching low to avoid the worst of the smoke. He collapsed onto the ground and the old man collapsed with him.

'Is he breathin'?' Tony shouted.

Karen looked closely at the old man. He had a bruise on his forehead and was quite still, but she could see his chest moving. As she leant close to him, thinking about the things she'd seen on telly, like the kiss of life, he grabbed her.

'Son, is that you? Where the bleeding hell did you go?'

'It's me, Karen, Mr Baldock.'

The old man looked at her blankly and began to cough, a low sound that seemed to come from the very heart of him. Something exploded inside the house. There was fire now. Flames were shooting up everywhere. Tiles started to explode on the roof.

'Get back!' shouted Tony. 'This is bloody dangerous.'

The fire brigade arrived, just as the end-terrace turned into an inferno. There was nothing much they could do, other than stop it spreading.

'This will all have to be rebuilt from scratch,' a fireman muttered as he passed by.

Karen clutched at the bodybuilder's arm.

'It was only the old man in there?' she shouted.

'I think so. I wasn't hanging round to find out. You couldn't see much anyway.'

'What a waste,' Tony said, 'all that dope up in smoke.'

Tony stood as close to the house as the firemen would allow and imagined he could smell the dope in the air. He breathed in deeply, and sighed.

Paramedics were also on the scene now, fussing over the bodybuilder's slight burns, and giving the old man oxygen. Tony held the bodybuilder's terrified dog. He expected the pigs to be along any minute too, and hoped all evidence would be well gone. Looking at the blazing house, he didn't doubt it.

'Will he be alright?' Karen shouted at a medic.

'Don't know yet, love. He's breathed in a lot of smoke and at his age ...' the man's voice tailed off as he looked up at Karen's face. Then he added, 'I know Mr Baldock, he was a friend of my father. He's a tough old bird.'

Karen nodded and moved away to let them do their work. Tony went with her. She leant against Tony as the dog growled at her. Karen repeatedly phoned Baldock's mobile but there was no answer.

'Oh Christ, you don't think Baldock was in there, do you, Tone?'

'Don' worry, love, I'm absolutely sure he wasn't.'

'How can you be?'

'Because here he is.'

Tony pointed his free hand down the street. Baldock was running towards them.

Chapter Fourteen

Baldock pushed through the crowd, almost knocking down a policeman in the process.

'Where you going, sunshine?' the cop asked.

'I live there!' Baldock shouted. 'Where's my father? Is he alright?'

The cop loosened his grip on Baldock's arm and helped him get forward. Baldock saw Karen, and Tony, and his father on a stretcher, about to be put into an ambulance.

'Dad! Dad! he's not ...'

'He's alive, Baldock,' Tony said. 'They think he's gonna be alright, but he's had a lot of smoke, like.'

Karen grabbed hold of Baldock.

'Where the hell have you been?' Karen shouted. 'And what have you been up to? Your face is covered in blood.'

Baldock touched his face with a hand and felt the crustiness of dried blood. It must have been when he'd felled TJ.

'Nothing. I'm alright.'

He pushed towards his father, who lay still

with an oxygen mask over his face. The old man's eyes opened when Baldock touched him on the shoulder. He motioned for Baldock to take off the mask. Baldock looked at a medic who nodded his head.

'You look bloody worse than me,' the old man whispered.

'I ran into a bush.'

'Aye, I'll believe you.'

'Dad, what happened?'

'I must have dozed off with a fag in my hand. An old man's trick. Next thing I know someone was carrying me down the stairs.' The old man coughed. 'Still, I've been taking in smoke and dust all my life. I'll handle this lot.'

'Course you will, Dad.'

'That's enough talk now,' the medic said, putting the mask back on Baldock's father. 'You can come in the ambulance with him if you want, mate.'

A fireman approached Baldock.

'You live here, I take it?'

'Yes.'

'Well, your father's been very lucky. The fire took a long time to get going. Only thing we can do now is make sure it's safe, it's too late to save anything.'

'Okay.'

Karen's face was close to Baldock's.

'TJ,' she whispered, 'you haven't ...?'

'He's okay. I didn't touch him. TJ's cool.'

Karen leant against him.

'Thanks, babe,' she whispered.

He wondered if she'd still thank him when she found out the full story.

Baldock turned to look at the house, or rather the shell of it. As the water hoses took effect it became a blackened hulk, with rafters exposed to the sky ...

The money! The fucking money! It hit him like a train. Like someone kicking him in the stomach. His stash. His profits of the last ten years. His first urge was to dash into the house. Baldock looked around wildly for the box, as if it might have been saved. There was no such miracle.

His legs were taking him closer to the house when a fireman stopped him.

'Hang on, mate. Don't get too near.'

'But ...'

But was all Baldock could say. His mouth was dry, he could feel his heart pounding, like it wanted to break through his ribs. Tony sidled up to him.

'Yeah, I know what you're thinking, boss.

All that dope going up in smoke. Must be a few hundred quid's worth.'

Baldock almost hit Tony. He could feel that old red mist closing in on him, but he couldn't afford to lose it here. There were police around, keeping back the crowd. No, losing it this time would have to be a private affair. Something to be kept inside, hoping he didn't explode.

Karen was talking to him.

'Come on, Baldock. They're taking your father now. I'll come with you.'

Baldock looked at her blankly.

'Baldock, snap out of it. I know it's a shock but your father's gonna be okay. Forget the house. It's only things, and if I know you, you'll be insured up to the hilt.'

He was, but how do you insure more than a hundred grand of illegal loot? Baldock screamed at himself inside. He'd planned to go to Switzerland in a few months, get someone to look after the old man and drive over there with the money. Find a bank where no questions were asked. He was always putting it off and it was too late now. Too late.

Karen pushed Baldock towards the ambulance and they got in with the old man. His father reached out a hand weakly and clasped Baldock's, beckoning him to come close and take off the oxygen mask again.

'Only for a few seconds,' the medic warned.

'Don't worry, son, I've had much worse than this,' the old man croaked. 'Like getting out of that blazing tank.'

Baldock nodded mechanically. Karen seemed to half guess his thoughts.

'Don't worry, love,' she said, 'I'm earning good money now. Plenty for us until your insurance comes through.'

'You sure you want it to be *us*?'

Karen leant closer to him and pressed her lips to his ear.

'Course I am,' she whispered. 'I was sure last night.'

As the ambulance sped away, the siren clearing its path, Baldock's hand closed on the money in his pocket. Five hundred quid. It was all he had left in the world. He was as wealthy and as poor as TJ. His head was spinning. He felt dizzy. Sick. He was thinking he'd have to start again, and was not sure how. He sat on the hard plastic seat in the ambulance and felt Karen's warm breath on his face as she snuggled up to him. He saw his father watching him, the old man's blue eyes still alert above his oxygen mask. Baldock closed his eyes, and suddenly felt free.

Quick Reads
Books in the Quick Reads series

www.quickreads.org.uk
www.quickreads.net

Quick Reads
The Hardest Test

Scott Quinnell

ACCENT PRESS

Scott Quinnell is one of the best-known names in rugby. He played both rugby league and rugby union, for Wales and for the British Lions. He was captain of the Welsh team seven times and won 52 caps.

But amidst all this success, Scott had a painful secret. He struggled to read. In *The Hardest Test*, he describes his struggle against learning difficulties throughout his childhood and his journey towards becoming one of the best rugby players in Britain. When he retired from rugby in 2005 he continued his battle with dyslexia in order to change both his and his children's lives.

Quick Reads
Life's New Hurdles

Colin Jackson

ACCENT PRESS

Colin Jackson is one of the greatest athletes that Britain has ever produced. He was in the world top ten for 16 years, and was world number 1 for two of them. He set seven European and Commonwealth and nine UK records and he still holds the world record for indoor hurdling.

In 2003, Colin retired from athletics in front of an adoring home crowd. Then real life began. In *Life's New Hurdles* Colin describes the shock of adjusting to sudden change. From athletics commentating to sports presenting and *Strictly Come Dancing*, Colin describes the challenges and joys of starting a whole new life.

Quick Reads
Vinyl Demand

Hayley Long

ACCENT PRESS

Beth Roberts and Rula Popek have a lot in common. They are both 19, both have crap jobs and both live in the worst flat in the whole of Wales.

The girls have no money, no boyfriends, family who are thousands of miles away and a final demand for a gas bill which they cannot pay. It all looks pretty bleak until one day when Rula stumbles across an entire vinyl record collection which has been left in a local charity shop. She takes a gamble and blows the money for the gas bill on the whole lot and the dream of becoming Cardiff's very own answer to the global girl DJ, Lisa Lashes. It's just a shame she didn't bother to explain the plan to Beth first.

Quick Reads

Aim High

Dame Tanni Grey Thompson

ACCENT PRESS

Aim High reveals what has motivated Dame Tanni Grey Thompson, UK's leading wheelchair athlete, through the highs and lows of her outstanding career. Her triumphs, which include winning 16 medals, eleven of which are gold, countless European titles, six London Marathons and over 30 world records have catapulted this Welsh wheelchair athlete firmly into the public consciousness.

Quick Reads
A Day To Remember

Fiona Phillips

ACCENT PRESS

A modern romantic comedy about love, loyalty and limos written by Fiona Phillips, GMTV presenter

A Day To Remember is a successful business but, when her right-hand man Steve runs away with their receptionist and the limo, Jo is left to pick up the pieces. Bookings are a mess, her home life's in chaos and then her son accidentally damages the new neighbour's Mercedes. Far from a Day To Remember it's turning into a week she'd just rather forget...

Quick Reads
Rubber Woman

Lindsay Ashford

ACCENT PRESS

Megan Rhys is a half-Welsh, half-Indian forensic psychologist who is assessing the impact of the government's new legislation on the vice trade in Cardiff. As predicted by critics, the problem hasn't gone away - prostitutes have simply moved into darker, more dangerous areas. Megan is deeply concerned about the risk this poses to the women - and her fears are justified when a prostitute is stabbed and left for dead. The story opens with Megan joining Pauline, a former prostitute turned outreach worker who the police called 'the oldest tart on the beat', in the red light district. Pauline is giving out condoms - she is affectionately known to the working girls as 'The Rubber Woman'.

Quick Reads
Bring It Back Home

Niall Griffiths

ACCENT PRESS

Chased by a hit-man, a young man returns home from London to a small town in Wales. Reconciliation with his family is alternated with his pursuer's progress. A long criminal connection is revealed but can he escape the sins of his fathers?

This is a tense, tightly written drama that will captivate the reader with fast, gut-wrenching action.

Quick Reads
The Corpse's Tale

Katherine John

ACCENT PRESS

Dai Morgan has the body of a man and the mind of a child. He lived with his mother in the Mid Wales village of Llan, next door to bright, beautiful 19 year old Anna Harris. The vicar found Anna's naked, battered body in the churchyard one morning. The police discovered Anna's bloodstained earring in Dai's pocket.

The judge gave Dai life.

After ten years in gaol Dai appealed against his sentence and was freed. Sergeants Trevor Joseph and Peter Collins are sent to Llan to reopen the case. But the villagers refuse to believe Dai innocent. The Llan police do not make mistakes or allow murderers to walk free.

Do they?

Quick Reads
Secrets

Lynne Barrett-Lee

ACCENT PRESS

Sisters Megan and Ffion have never had secrets, so when Megan goes to flat-sit all she's expecting is a rest and a change.

When a stranger called Jack phones, Megan wonders who he is. Ffion behaves like she's just seen a ghost, and refuses to say any more.

So is Jack a ghost? Ffion's not telling and when she disappears too, the mystery deepens. Megan begins to fear for the future. She's always been the one who has looked after her little sister. Is this going to be the one time she can't?